Hamlin Garland

Prairie Songs

Being Chants Rhymed and Unrhymed of the Level Lands of the Great West

Hamlin Garland

Prairie Songs
Being Chants Rhymed and Unrhymed of the Level Lands of the Great West

ISBN/EAN: 9783744774031

Printed in Europe, USA, Canada, Australia, Japan

Cover: Foto ©Andreas Hilbeck / pixelio.de

More available books at **www.hansebooks.com**

PRAIRIE SONGS

BEING CHANTS RHYMED AND
UNRHYMED OF THE LEVEL
LANDS OF THE GREAT WEST
BY HAMLIN GARLAND WITH
DRAWINGS BY H. T. CARPENTER

CAMBRIDGE AND CHICAGO
PUBLISHED BY STONE AND
KIMBALL IN THE YEAR
MDCCCXCIII

TO MY BROTHER FRANKLIN
IN MEMORY OF THE PRAIRIES
OVER WHICH WE RODE TOGETHER

FOREWORD

OST modern men, I fancy, find it rather difficult to take verse (not poetry) seriously. It is so restrictive and so monotonous in comparison with the flexibility of prose, that it forever hampers and binds in the man's larger feeling Prose seems to be drawing off all that is most modern and freest and most characteristic of our American civilization. I do not expect, therefore, to have these verses taken to represent my larger work.

A quarter of a century ago the prairies of Northern Iowa were only just won from the elk and buffalo, whose bones and antlers lay in thousands beside every trail and watering place. These rich and splendid meadows had swarmed with herbivora for ages of undisturbed possession, and every crumbling crib of bones or bleaching antler was a powerful incentive to a boy's imagination. From them my mind was able to construct some idea of the grandeur of the flocks which once peopled these green vistas. Even then I felt the beauty of the wilderness, which is coming to have deeper charm as it passes irrecoverably from sight.

The prairies are not the plains. The plains do not begin until you reach the Missouri river and begin to climb toward the Rocky Mountains. These verses have to do with both plains and prairies, though the wild prairies are nearly gone. The vegetation differs wildly, as will be evident from allusions throughout this volume. The plains are mainly clothed in a short hair-like grass which cures early in the stock and is russet in color during most of the year.

The prairies were rich in grasses. Blue-joint, crows-foot and wild oats. Sunflowers and innumerable and brilliant flowers grew in the beautiful meadows, out of which groves of popple and hazel bushes rose like islands out of shallow seas.

These prairies were intersected by beautiful streams, belted in splendid groves of oaks and maples and basswood trees. The prairies were generally level, with long swells like a quiet sea, but in the neighborhood of streams they grew more varied and wooded.

Over such prairie grasses, around such tow-heads of popple trees, my brother and I rode, racing with half-wild horses, chasing the wild fox and the prairie wolf, spying out the Massasauga in the grass, and munching hazel nuts in lee of hazel thickets on cold November days. Those were glorious days !

I have lived many phases of life, but those few

years among the colts and cattle of the prairies, before settlement closed the cows' wild pasture and stabled the horses, are among my happiest recollections.

The prairies are gone. I held one of the ripping, snarling, breaking plows that rolled the hazel bushes and the wild sunflowers under. I saw the wild steers come into pasture and the wild colts come under harness. I saw the wild fowl scatter and turn aside; I saw the black sod burst into gold and lavender harvests of wheat and corn—and so there comes into my reminiscences an unmistakable note of sadness. I do not excuse it or conceal it. I set it down as it comes to me. I have designedly excluded all things alien to the book and its title. I make no further claim than this;—it is composed of prairie songs.   HAMLIN GARLAND.

A TABLE OF THE CONTENTS OF THIS BOOK.

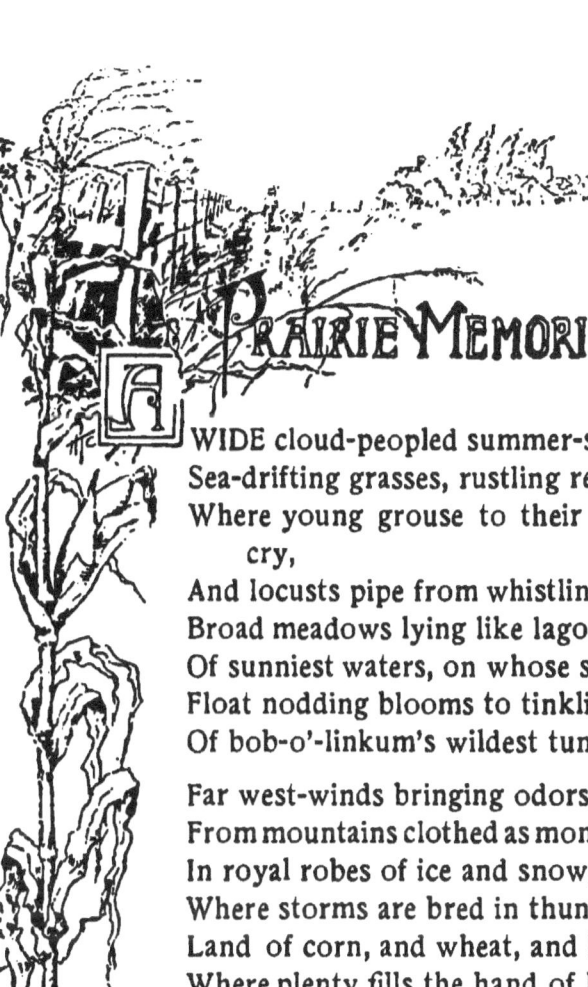

PRAIRIE MEMORIES

A WIDE cloud-peopled summer-sky;
Sea-drifting grasses, rustling reeds,
Where young grouse to their mothers
    cry,
And locusts pipe from whistling weeds;
Broad meadows lying like lagoons
Of sunniest waters, on whose swells
Float nodding blooms to tinkling bells
Of bob-o'-linkum's wildest tunes;

Far west-winds bringing odors, fresh
From mountains clothed as monarchs are
In royal robes of ice and snow,
Where storms are bred in thunder-jar;
Land of corn, and wheat, and kine,
Where plenty fills the hand of him
Who tills the soil or prunes the vine
Or digs in thy far canons dim—

My Western land, I love thee yet!
In dreams I ride my horse again
And breast the breezes blowing fleet
From out the meadows cool and wet.

From fields of flowers blowing sweet,
And flinging perfume to the breeze.
The wild oats swirl along the plain;
I feel their dash against my knees,
Like rapid plash of running seas.

I pass by islands, dark and tall,
Of slender poplars thick with leaves;
The grass in rustling ripple, cleaves
To left and right in emerald flow;
And as I listen, riding slow,
Out breaks the wild bird's jocund call.

Oh, shining suns of boyhood's time !
Oh, winds that from the mythic west
Sang calls to Eldorado's quest !
Oh, swaying wild bird's thrilling chime !
When the loud city's clanging roar
Wraps in my soul as if in shrouds
I hear those sounds and songs once more,
And dream of boyhood's wind-swept clouds

THE WEST WIND.

Oh! the wind is abroad in the hollows
And a-sweep on the swells of the plain,
Where the dun grass tosses and wallows,
And the hazel bush shakes as in pain—
    With a petulant air and a shiver
    Of fright and of pain—
While the broad breeze streams like a river
And roars like a far-off main.

The wide waves, restless, but weary,
Roll on to the half-hid sun.
Hear the rush!
    Hear the roar!
        Hear the murmur!
See the swift waves serially run,
Like fowls from the eagle's swift wings!
To the bowed ear's hearing, there comes
The sound of far harping of harp strings,
The noise of dim pipings and drums.

Oh! magic west wind of the prairie!
    How he leaps in his might!
No boundaries knows he or cares he,
    No day and no night.
His footsteps grow weary never,
    He is here!
        He is there!
Now he harries the clouds in the air,
Now he tramples the grass in his flight.

But whether in spring or in summer,
Or in autumn's gray shadow or shine,
Chainless and care-free is he
As a faun in a riot of wine.
He is lord of the whole sky's hollow;
He possesses the whole vast plain;
He leads and the wild clouds follow—
He frowns and they vanish in rain!

COMING RAIN
ON THE PRAIRIE

IN SOUNDING southern breeze
The spire-like poplar trees
    Stream like vast plumes
Against a seamless cloud—a high
Dark mass, a dusty dome that looms
A rushing shadow on the western sky.

The lightning falls in streams,
Sprangling in fiery seams,
    Through which the bursting rain
Falls in trailing clouds of gray;
The cattle draw together on the plain,
And drift like anchored boats upon a wind-swept
    bay.

MASSASAUGA—THE MEADOW RATTLESNAKE.

A cold coiled line of mottled lead,
He lies where grazing cattle tread
And lifts a fanged and spiteful head.

His touch is deadly, and his eyes
Are hot with hatred and surprise—
Death waits and watches where he lies!

His hate is turned toward everything!
He is the undisputed king
Of every path and woodland spring.

His naked fang is raised to smite
All passing things; light
Is not swifter than his bite.

His touch is deadly, and his eyes
Are hot with hatred and surprise—
Death waits and watches where he lies!

SPRING on the PRAIRIE

AND the fields grew green
      With the mighty mystery
   Of springing grain;
The poplar trees burst into yellow leaf,
The oak leaves pricked like a squirrel's ear,
And in the mellow grounds the planter strode;
The birds paired off and nested,
The horses fed on the sunny slopes
Where the crocus bloomed and the early grasses
Yielded their sweets to the cattle's lips;
And like some peerless overture, the vast
Sweet symphony the wild chickens sang at dawn
Died away to a single note,
And genial spring was merged in sultry summer.

A SONG OF WINDS.

Winds from the prairies where wild weeds shiver;
Winds from the popple trees' quick leaves' quiver,
Where the blithe chickens boom and shrill frogs
    chime—
O winds from my boyhood's far-away time,
I wait for you, long for you, here in the town!

Filled with the memory of grasses and trees,
I long for my prairies as a sailor loves seas;
I hear in red mornings the wild chickens calling,
I hear at still nooning the bugle note falling
From crane sweeping by in the fathomless sky.

I long, oh! I long to lie in the stubble,
Close by the creek, where the cool waters bubble;
Longing to lose in a dream all my care,
Feeling the summer winds kissing my hair,
Hearing the willows shake over my head!

INDIAN SUMMER

T LAST there came
 The sudden fall of frost,
  when Time
Dreaming through russet September days
Suddenly awoke, and lifting his head, strode
Swiftly forward—made one vast desolating sweep
Of his scythe, then, rapt with the glory
That burned under his feet, fell dreaming again.
And the clouds soared and the crickets sang
In the brief heat of noon; the corn,
So green, grew sere and dry—
  And in the mist the ploughman's team
  Moved silently, as if in dream—
And it was Indian summer on the plain.

COLOR IN THE WHEAT.

Like liquid gold the wheat field lies,
A marvel of yellow and green,
That ripples and runs, that floats and flies,
With the subtle shadows, the change—the sheen
That plays in the golden hair of a girl.
A cloud flies there—
A ripple of amber—a flare
Of light follows after. A swirl
In the hollows like the twinkling feet
Of a fairy waltzer, the colors run
To the western sun,
Through the deeps of the ripening wheat.

I hear the reapers' far-off hum,
So faint and far, it seems the drone
Of bee or beetle; seems to come
From far-off, fragrant, fruity zone,
A land of plenty, where,
Toward the sun, as hasting there,
The colors run before the wind's feet
In the wheat.

The wild hawk swoops
To his prey in the deeps;
The sun-flower droops
To the lazy wave; the wind sleeps—
Then running in dazzling links and loops
A marvel of shadow and shine,
A glory of olive and amber and wine
Runs the color in the wheat.

THE MEADOW LARK

A BRAVE little bird that fears
    not God,
    A voice that breaks from the
    snow-wet clod
With prophecy of sunny sod,
Set thick with wind-waved golden-rod.

From the first bare clod in the raw cold spring,
From the last bare clod, when fall winds sting,
The farm-boy hears his brave song ring,
And work for the time is a pleasant thing.

THE HUSH OF THE PLAINS—JULY.

As some vast orchestra, listening, waits
Full-breathed and tense in a sudden lull,
With only the string-bass throbbing on,
Ready at fall of the leader's wand
To break into soft, slow swell,
So the plain lies, hushed and dumb as death,
Songless and soundless.

No crickets fill the pause with whirr,
No bird wakes a note or stirs a wing.
Only the flute-like note of the lark sounds,
Only the flashing, inaudible wing of the gull moves,
All else waits, listens.
Only the wide wind droning on,
Wide as the plain, vaguely vast,
The string-bass throbbing dimly on.

PIONEERS

HEY rise to mastery of
wind and snow;
They go like soldiers grimly
into strife
To colonize the plain. They plow and sow,
And fertilize the sod with their own life,
As did the Indian and the buffalo.

SETTLERS.

Above them soars a dazzling sky,
 In winter blue and clear as steel,
In summer like an arctic sea,
 Wherein great icebergs drift and reel
 And melt like sudden sorcery;

Beneath them plains stretch far and fair,
 Rich with sunlight and with rain;
Vast harvests ripen with their care
 And fill with overplus of grain
 Their square great bins;

Yet still they strive! I see them rise
 At dawn-light going forth to toil;
The same salt sweat has filled my eyes;
 My feet have trod the self-same soil
 Behind the snarling share.

PRAIRIE FIRES.

A curving, leaping line of light,
A crackling roar from lurid lungs,
A wild flush on the skies of night—
A force that gnaws with hot red tongues,
That leaves a blackened smoking sod—
A fiery furnace where the cattle trod.

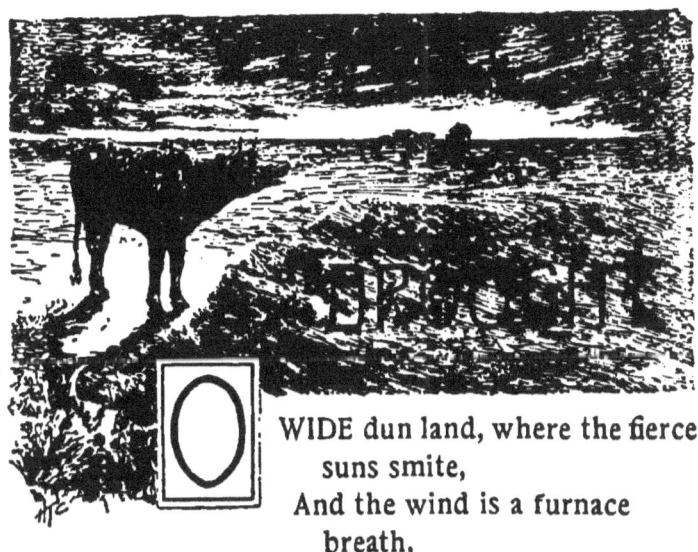

O WIDE dun land, where the fierce
suns smite,
And the wind is a furnace
breath,
Where the beautiful sky has a sinister light,
And the earth lies dread and dry as death;
Where the sod lies scorching and wan grass sighs,
And the hot red morning has no birds—
O songless sunset land! I close mine eyes
In sheer despair of thy dim reach—
O level waste! so lone thou art, no words
Can tell, no pictures teach.

A presence like a curse! no insects hum—
No chirping crickets' cheery ring—
A white mist-wall of bounding space
Flecked with the swift gull's fluttering,
Alone confronts the asking face!
No tree stands green against the sky—
The hawk swims in the blazing air,
He scarce can find (though keen his eye)
A human heart beat anywhere.

So hot and lone the plain—O God!
The very breezes faint and die
Along the burning hopeless sod
Where sere grass rustles sullenly.
All creatures turn an asking eye
To where the radiant heavens soar
In cloudless splendor—a cry
Bursts from the bitten lip—deathwise
The desperate husbandmen, with hands
Outspread, clutch at the dust.
Their harvest withers where it stands
And burns to ashes while they trust!

AT DUSK

NDOLENT I lie
Beneath the sky
Thick-sown with clouds that soar and float
Like stately swans upon the air,
And in the hush of dusk I hear
The ring-dove's plaintive liquid note
Sound faintly as a prayer.

Against the yellow sky
The grazing kine stalk slowly by;
Like wings that spread and float and flee
The clouds are drifting over me.
The couching cattle sigh,
And from the meadow damp and dark
I hear the piping of the lark;
While falling night-hawks scream and boom,
Like rockets, through the rising gloom,
And katydids with pauseless chime
Bear on the far frogs' ringing rhyme.

A WINTER BROOK.

How sweetly you sang as you circled
  The elm's rugged knees in the sod,
I know! for deep in the shade of your willows,
  A barefooted boy with a rod,
I lay in the drowsy June weather,
  And sleepily whistled in tune
To the laughter I heard in your shallows,
  Involved with the music of June !

THE VOICE OF THE PINES.

Wailing, wailing,
O ceaseless wail of the pines.
Sighing, sighing,
An incommunicable grief!

No matter how bright the summer sky,
No matter how the dandelions star the sod,
Nor how the bees buzz in the cherry blooms,
Nor how the rich green grass is thick with daisies,
While the sun moves through the dazzling sky,
And the up-rolled clouds sail slowly on,
The nun-voiced pines, sombre and strong,
Breathe on their endless moaning song.

The birds do not dwell there or sing there !
They fly to trees with fruit and shining leaves,
Where twigs swing gayly and boughs are in bloom—
Among these glooms they would surely die,
And their young forget to swing and sway.
The wild hawk may sit here and scream;
The gray-coated owl utter his hoarse note;
And the dark ravens perch and peer,
But the robins, the orioles, the bright singers
Flee these sighing pines.

Sighing, sighing !
O vast illimitable voice !
Like the moan of multitudes, the chant of nuns,
Thy ceaseless wail and cry comes on me.

And when the autumn sky is dull and wild,
When jagged clouds stream swiftly by,
When the sleet falls in slant torrents,
When thy dripping arms, outspread, are drear
And harsh with cold and rain,
Then thy voice, O pines, is stern and wild;
Thy sigh becomes a vengeful moan and snarl—
A voice of stormy, inexpressible anguish
Timed to the sweep of thy tossing boughs,
Keyed to the desolate gray of the ragged sky.

       Wailing, wailing !
    O vast illimitable wail of the pines !
The chill wash of swift dark streams,
The joyless days, the lonely nights,
Hungry noons, funeral trains, with trappings of
      sable,—
The burial chants with clods falling in the grave—
All the measureless and eternal inheritance of grief
All the ineffable woe which has oppressed my race
All the tragedy I have felt
With all that my ancestors have felt,
Comes back to me here,
Borne on the wings of thine eternal wail,
Blent in the flow
Of thine incommunicable sorrow.

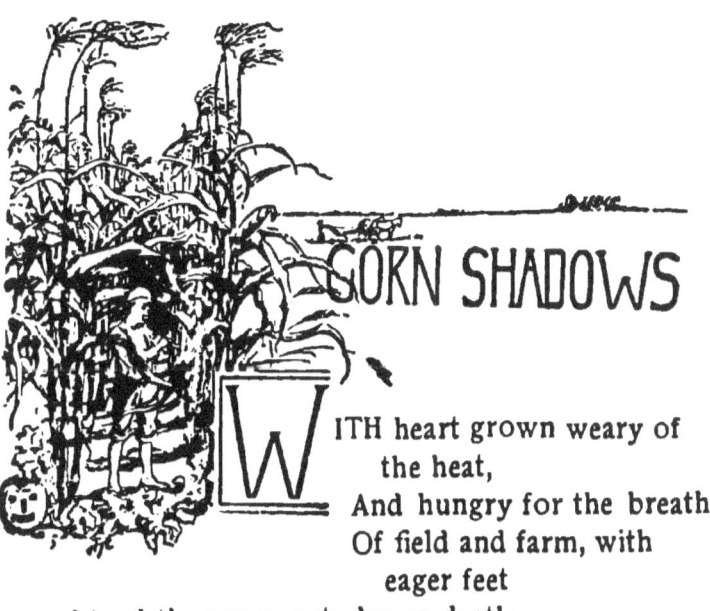

CORN SHADOWS

WITH heart grown weary of
the heat,
And hungry for the breath
Of field and farm, with
eager feet
I trod the pavement, dry as death,
Through city streets where vice is born—
And sudden, lo! a ridge of corn!

Above the dingy roofs it stood,
A dome of tossing tangled spears,
Dark, cool, and sweet as any wood
Its silken green and plumed ears
Laughed on me through the haze of morn
The tranquil presence of the corn.

Upon the salt wind from the sea
Borne westward swift as dreams
Of boyhood are, I seemed to be
Once more a part of sounds and gleams
Thrown on me by the winds of morn
Amid the rustling rows of corn.

39

I bared my head, and on me fell
The old wild wizardry again
Of leaf and sky, the moving spell
Of boyhood's easy joy or pain,
When pumpkin trump was Siegfried's horn
Echoing down the walls of corn.

I saw the field (as trackless then
As wood to Daniel Boone)
Wherein we hunted wolves and men
And ranged and twanged the green bassoon—
(Not blither Robin Hood's merry horn
Than pumpkin vine amid the corn!)

In central deeps the melons lay
Slow swelling in the August sun.
I traced again the narrow way
And joined again the stealthy run—
The jack-o'-lantern wraith was born
Within the shadows of the corn.

O wide, west wilderness of leaves!
O playmates, far away! over thee
The slow wind like a mourner grieves
And stirs the plumed ears like a sea.
Would we could sound again the horn
In vast sweet presence of the corn!

THE HERALD
CRANE

H! say, you so, bold sailor
   In the sun-lit deeps of sky!
Dost thou so soon the seed-time tell
   In thy imperial cry,
As circling in yon shoreless sea
   Thine unseen form goes drifting by?

I can not trace in the noon-day glare
   Thy regal flight, O crane!
From the leaping might of the fiery light
   Mine eyes recoil in pain,
But on mine ear, thine echoing cry
   Falls like a bugle strain.

The mellow soil glows beneath my feet,
   Where lies the buried grain;
The warm light floods the length and breadth
   Of the vast, dim, shimmering plain,
Throbbing with heat and the nameless thrill
   Of the birth-time's restless pain.

On weary wing, plebeian geese
Push on their arrowy line
Straight into the north, or snowy brant
In dazzling sunshine, gloom and shine;
But thou, O crane, save for thy sovereign cry,
At thy majestic height
On proud, extended wings sweep'st on
In lonely, easeful flight.

Then cry, thou martial-throated herald !
Cry to the sun, and sweep
And swing along thy mateless, tireless course
Above the clouds that sleep
Afloat on lazy air—cry on !   Send down
Thy trumpet note—it seems
The voice of hope and dauntless will,
And breaks the spell of dreams.

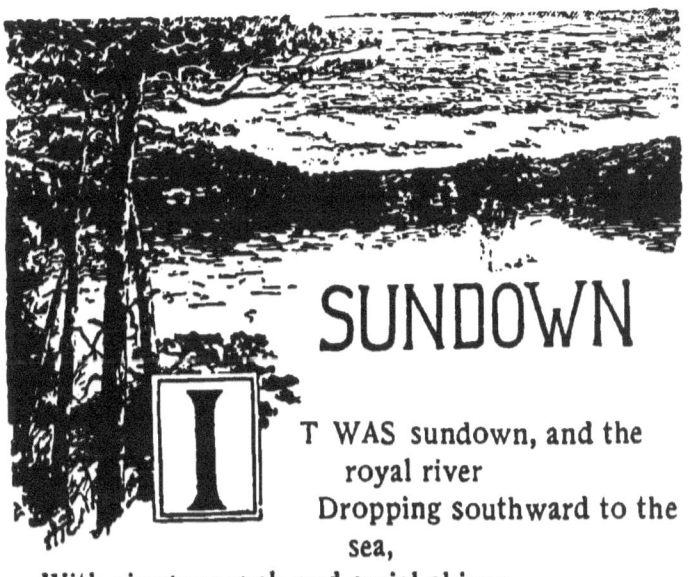

SUNDOWN

IT WAS sundown, and the royal river
  Dropping southward to the sea,
With rippling rush and serial shiver
Of small waves in the reedy sedges,
Swept round its yellow limestone ledges;
And the far-off pulsing came to me
Of a negro boatman's melody.
  Like a silvery wind-blown vail
The shimmering mist lay on the heights,
Struck through and through by the level shafts
Of the rising, spotless orange moon.
The bittern boomed from the shadowy marsh,
The curlew piped in lonesome cry,
And the frogs from the river made reply.
  The mass and depth and mystery
Of the river deepened, till its flood
Seemed magical. Its weight of dark
Unresting waters was so swift, so broad,
It seemed as if some prisoned sea
Were slipping by me hurriedly.

IN THE AUTUMN GRASS.

Did you ever lie low
In the depth of the plain,
In the lee of a swell that lifts
Like a low-lying island out of the sea,
  When the blue joint shakes
    As an army of spears;
  When each flashing wave breaks
  In turn overhead
    And wails in the door of your ears?

If you have, you have heard
  In the midst of the roar,
The note of a lone gray bird,
Blown slantwise by overhead
As he swiftly sped
  To his south-land haven once more!

O the music abroad in the air,
With the autumn wind sweeping
His hand on the grass, where
The tiniest blade is astir, keeping
Voice in the dim, wide choir,
Of the infinite song, the refrain,
The wild, sad wail of the plain!

DREAMS OF THE GRASS.

O ! to lie in long grasses !
    O ! to dream on the plain !
Where the west wind sings as it passes,
    A weird and unceasing refrain !
Where the rank grass tosses and wallows,
    And the plain's rim dazzles the eye
Where hardly a silver cloud bosses
    The flashing steel shield of the sky !

To watch the gay gulls as they glitter
    Like snowflakes, and fall from on high
To dip in the deeps of the prairie;
    Where the crows foot tosses awry,
        Like the swirl o' swift waltzers in glee,
To the harsh, shrill creak of the cricket
    And the song of the lark and the bee !

MEADOW MEMORIES.

O Memory, what conjury is thine!
Once more the sun shines on the wneat—
Once more I drink the wind like wine
When bursts the lark's song wildly-sweet
From out the rain-wet, new-mown grass;
I hear the sickle's clattering sweep,
And peals of laughter swell and pass
From lip to lip; again I heap
The odorous wind-rows, rank by rank.
Silent the rancuous tumult of the street—
From iron pavements ceaseless clank,
From grinding hooves and jar of car
I flee, and lave my boyish feet
Where bee-lodged clover blossoms are!

THE WHIP-POOR-WILL'S HOUR.

The cool sweet air,
The dark fern-scented woods,
The breath of oak and pine,
The fire-flies in the grass,
The chirp of sleepy crickets,
The song of the thrush,
A lullaby of streams,
The unutterable coolness and sweetness—
The odor of apple blooms and grass—
Then   from the fragrant dusk of pines
The whip-poor-will puts forth his slender cry.

A SUMMER MOOD.

O, to be lost in the wind and the sun,
    To be one with the wind and the stream!
With never a care while the waters run
    With never a thought in my dream.
To be part of the robin's lilting call
    And part of the bobolink's rhyme.
Lying close to the shy thrush singing alone,
    And lapped in the cricket's chime.

O, to live with these beautiful ones !
    With the lust and the glory of man
Lost in the circuit of spring-time suns—
    Submissive as earth and part of her plan—
To lie as the snake lies, content in the grass !
    To drift as the clouds drift, effortless, free,
Glad of the power that drives them on
    With never a question of wind or sea.

ATAVISM

SOMETIMES, ranging the
upland sod,
A lean, lone steer comes
suddenly upon
A trace of blood.—Like a hound he stops
And wheels, snuffling the earth.
His eyes roll savagely, his nostrils expand
And his wrinkled neck stiffens. He paws
The ground with horny hoofs. He lifts
His voice in a wild roar that ends
In a harsh scream.

The herd listens, still as statues—
Every horn lifted, every nostril spread!—
Again it comes, that screaming roar,
Wild as the tiger's food-sick cry!
A score of voices echo it, and then
The whole herd wakes to action.
The plain swarms with flying forms
Centering with savage, menacing run
Towards the bawling sentinel.

The noise becomes frightful—
Every curling tongue joins the sudden tumult—
Lions are not more terrible of voice.
The domestic is lost in savagery.
The snorting, bawling roar of heavy-uddered cows,
Proclaims the power of memory.
All frantic with roused memory of war
And fear and hate of man and wolf,
They rush in ranks like warriors.
Their tails wave like pennon lances.

The herdsman dreaming beneath the shine
Of poplar trees, springs to his saddle
And sits wondering, while his horse
With nostrils blown like trumpets,
Fronts the scene, his eyes
Reflecting the storm-like rush
                    Of the trampling herd.

            The bulls paw the earth;
Their eyes roll and flame from the dust
Their hollow hoofs have raised—
The herd surges to and fro in mass,
Blind and savage, seeking an unseen cause
Of some ancestral danger.

IN A LULL IN THE SPLENDORS OF BRAHMS.

In a lull in the splendors of Brahms,
When the passionate wail of the flute,
Struck dumb by the stroke of the drums,
Like the voice of a child sank mute:
In tbe second 'twixt thunder and thunder,
In the hush ere the wild music came
My soul flew far to the plain
Where the blue sky arched, and wide land under
Rolled a sea of grasses and growing grain.

II.

I lay in the reeds of the prairie,
In the hush of the night, and I heard
The wandering wind, swift and wary,
Slipping by in the grass like a snake.
Faint clouds floated high in the air—
A lone wolf howled on a swell—
A bird in the grass seemed to tremble and wake,
And sent on the chime of the crickets afloat,
A clear and most marvelous note
That lay in the ear like a prayer.

III.

The dim moon set!
The wolf ceased his cry.
Overhead the far meteors streamed redly,
And dropped down the dark
Southern dome of the sky—
The chime of the hid cricket stopped
As if awed by strange sounds in the air—
And then, as I waited in trance of desire,
With throbbing shut eyes,
The ear was aware
Of stir in the wide waste of grasses; a glare
Overshot the gray East with red fire—
With swelling vague clamor,
Swift beat and shrill blare
Back to the hearing the deep music came,
As out of the darkness a vast army comes,
Roaring like wind and wild flame
To burst in the thunder of drums!

THE PASSING
OF THE BUFFALO

GOING the wild things of our
        land,
Passing the antelope and buffalo.
They have gone with the sunny sweep
        Of the untracked plain!
They have passed away with the untrammeled
    current of our streams!

    With the falling trees they fell,
    With the autumn grass they rotted,
    And their bones
    Lie white on the flame-charred sod,
    Mixed with antlers of the elk.

For centuries they lay down and rose
        In peace and calm content.
They were fed by the rich grass
And watered by sunny streams.
The plover called to them
        Out of the shimmering air,

The hawk swooped above them,
The blackbird sat on their backs
   In the still afternoons,
In the cool mud they wallowed,
   Rolling in noisy sport.

They lived through centuries of struggle—
In swarming millions—till the white man came.
The snows of winter were terrible!
The dry wind was hard to bear,
But the breath of man, the smoke
   Of his gun was more fatal.

   They fell by thousands.
   They melted away like smoke!
Mile by mile they retreated westward;
Year by year they moved north and south
   In dust-brown clouds;
Each year they descended upon the plains
   In endless floods;
Each winter they retreated to the hills
   Of the south.
Their going was like the ocean current,
But each spring they stopped a little short—
They were like an ebbing tide!
They came at last to meager little bands
   That never left the hills—
Crawling in sombre files from canon to canon—
   Now, they are gone!

O the unfenced vistas of sod
    They fed upon!
O the sweet strange memories they evoke!
The sun-lit prairie with groves and streams,
The rich grasses, the undisturbed primeval wild—
    All gone, all gone!
    Swallowed up, lost irretrievably.
    My heart aches with longing for it.

    Gone the wild turkey!
    Gone the deer and antelope!
Passing the crane and the prairie chicken!
    Passing the wild free spaces
That swarmed with feet and echoed with bawl
Of bulls and savage snarl of wolves—
    Ended the infinite drama of savage life.

    Passing the seas of hazel-brush;
    Passing the prairie sod
And all its wealth of grass and flowers,
    The swirling crow's foot.
    The tossing plumes of snake weed,
    The golden groves of sunflowers,
        Passing, never to return.

O the regret of it.
O the mystery and power
    Of the untracked land,
The lure of winds from unknown spaces,
The wonder and power of swift rivers,
Where only the shy beaver builds a dam—
O wild woods and rivers and untrod sweep of sod!

I exult that I have known you!
I have felt you and worshiped you!
I cannot be robbed of the memory
        Of horse and plain
        And bird and flower,
Nor the song of the illimitable west wind.
        They are all part of my life,
        And while I live they will endure.
When I am old my heart will thrill,
And I will say, I saw the wild sod burst
To blossom, before the city's trample
        Drowned the winds' sweet song!

AN APOLOGY.

The ancient minstrel when times befit,
And his song outran his laggard pen,
Went forth in the world and chanted it
In the market place, to the busy men;
Who found full leisure to listen and long
For the far-off land of the minstrel's song.

Let me play minstrel and sing the lines
Which rise in my heart in praise of the plain!
I'll lead you where the wild oat shines,
And swift clouds dapple the wheat with rain.
If you'll listen, you'll hear the songs of birds
And the shuddering roar of trampling herds.

The brave brown lark from the russet sod
Will pipe as clear as a cunning flute,
Though sky and sod are stern as God,
And the wind and plain lie hot and mute—
Though the gulls complain of the blazing air
And the grass lies brown and crisp as hair.

HOME FROM THE CITY.

Out of the city, out of the street!
Out in the wind and the grasses,
Where the bird and the daisy wooing meet,
And the cloud like an eagle passes.
Far from the roaring street.

Out of the hurry, away from the heat
And clamor of iron wheels and hooves,
Out of the stench and scorching heat
We come as a dove to its native roofs,
Far from the thunderous street.

Into the silence of cool-breathed leaves,
Where the wind like a lover
Murmurs, and waits to listen, and weaves
His arms in the leafy cover—
Back to a world of stubble and sheaves
We flee from the murderous street!

APRIL DAYS.

Days of witchery subtly sweet,
  When every hill and tree finds heart;
When winter and spring like lovers meet
  In the mist of noon and part—
    In the April days.

Nights when the wood-frogs faintly peep—
  One, *two*, and then are still,
And the woodpeckers' martial voices sweep
  Like bugle blasts from hill to hill
    Through the breathless morn.

Days when the soil is warm with rain,
  And through the wood the shy wind steals,
Rich with the pine and the poplar smell,
  And the joyous brain like a dancer reels
    Through April days.

BY THE RIVER.

A sun-lit stream
Flows athwart my dream,
With a gurgle of laughter in sunny shallows,
    Where rounded boulders, white and red,
    On a pebbly bed
    Lie wide bespread,
With shoulders and hollows,
Smoothed down and scooped out
By the swift water's rout.

It comes from the meadow,
    Where cool and deep   .
In the elm's dark shadow,
    In murmur of dream and of sleep
        It drowsily eddied and swirled,
        And softly crept and curled
            Round the out-thrust knees
            Of the white-wood trees,
        And lifted the rustling dripping sedge
    In rhythmic sweep at the outer edge.

There the graceful water-snake rippled across
Through the shimmering dapple the leaves cast
    down,
While the swamp-bird, perched on the spongy moss
At the darker side, looked gravely on.
It was there the kingfisher swiftly flew
In the cool sweet silence from tree to tree—

All silent, save when the vagabond jay
Flashed swiftly by with wild *tchee!*—
Swaggering by in his elfish way.

The hot dust drifts along the street
And fills the air with a furnace heat,
    Stifling the crowds of hurrying men,
But in my dreaming and rippling rhyme
It is noon in the sultriest summer time,
    And I, a bare-legged boy again,
Can hear the low sweet laugh of the river,
See on the water the dapples a-quiver,
    Feel on my knees the lipping-lap
Of the sunny ripples, see the snake
Slip silently into the sedgy brake,
    And hear the rising pickerel slap
        With a rushing leap
        Where the lilies sleep!

A MOUNTAIN-SIDE.

A height that curved like a woman's breast,
A stream that plunged in mad unrest
Through sullen snow and gray-green grass,
And fell a thousand feet
      Below the mountain pass.

Its wild roar mingled with the moan
Of snarling pines, rooted on mottled stone;
The gray clouds blurred the'saffron peaks with
    snow
Ten thousand feet above the vale below.

IN AUGUST

ROM the great trees the locusts
cry
In quavering ecstatic duo—a
boy
Shouts a wild call—a mourning dove
In the blue distance sobs—the wind
Wanders by, heavy with odors
Of corn and wheat and melon vines;
The trees tremble with delirious joy as the
breeze
Greets them, one by one—now the oak,
Now the great sycamore, now the elm.

And the locusts in brazen chorus, cry
Like stricken things, and the ring-dove's note
Sobs on in the dim distance.

THE BLUE JAY.

His eye is bright as burnished steel,
  His note a quick defiant cry;
Harsh as a hinge his grating squeal
  Sounds from the keen wind sweeping by.

Rains never dim his smooth blue coat,
  The winter never troubles him.
No fog puts hoarseness in his throat
  Or makes his merry eyes grow dim.
His cry at morning is a shout.—
  His wing is subject to his heart.
Of fear he knows not—doubt
  Did not draw his sailing-chart.

He is an universal emigre;
  His foot is set in every land.
He greets me by gray Casco bay,
  And laughs across the Texas sand.
In heat or cold, in storm or sun
  He lives unfearingly, and when he dies
He folds his feet up one by one
  And turns a last look at the skies.

He is the true American! He fears
  No journey and no wood or wall,
And in the desert, toiling voyagers
  Take heart of courage from his call.

THE MOUNTAINS

EVER the mountains face the plain,
Ever the plainsman's longing
    eyes
Turn to the distant peaks.

In the warm mornings, when the lark
Whistles from cool, sage-green, close-curling grass,
When not a cloud stains the sky—
Then the mountains stand forth
        Warm, sharply outlined,
Wearing a time-worn cloak of purple rock
  .   And dark green pines.

They draw near the plain,
They seem close, intimate, prosaic.
Every hollow and wrinkle is displayed,
Every rasp and ravage of wind and frost
Is seen, every canon seems emptied
        Of its mystery and color.

But as the sun swings west,
A splendid robe of royal blue
    Drops over the distant peaks,
And lowers and deepens
    And grows richer and richer
Till the whole mighty group is arrayed
In purple splendid distance.

They withdraw into color and depth
    Like demigods;
They lift their heads like those
    Who wear crowns;
They begin at the plainsman's feet,
    They end in space where dreams are,
        Where scars become heroic history,
        Where silence reigns in majesty like death
     `As the sun sinks,
        The canons deepen in color,
Adding mystery to silence. They become awful
    deeps
Where stupendous cats and great birds
        Move about the strange walls
        Carved and hollowed by water.
        Caves yawn wider as night thickens.

The lone traveler, lying beneath
The silent pines on some high range,
Watches and listens in ecstacy of fear
        And exalted admiration.

The prosaic is gone,
The present is gone,
The eastern plain becomes an obscure sea,
Its life absorbed by distance—
He is alone with the stupendous, the inexorable,
The past!

In the roar of the far stream
   Is the reminiscent dream
      Of colossal cataracts;
In the cry of the cliff-bird, he hears
   The scream of the eagle
      Or the yawl of the mountain lion;
In the fall of a loose rock
He fancies he hears the stealthy tread of the grizzly;
In the black night of the lower canon,
He thinks he sees once more
Prodigious lines of buffaloes,
   Or files of Indian armies
Winding downward to the distant valley
   Where camp-fires shine like stars—

         And the dreamer shudders
         With a strange longing thrill,
         A regret for the vanished past.
         He trembles—but to tremble here
         Is not fear—it is comprehension!

MY CABIN.

My cabin cowers in the onward sweep
  Of the terrible northern blast;
Above its roof the wild clouds leap,
  And shriek as they hurry past.
The snow-waves hiss along the plain,
Like hungry wolves they stretch and strain.
They race and romp with rushing beat;
Like stealthy tread of myriad feet
They pass the door.   Upon the roof
  The icy showers swirl and rattle.
At times the moon, though far aloof,
  Through winds and snow in furious battle,
Shines white and wan within the room—
  Then swift clouds dart across the light,
  And all the plain is lost to sight;
  The cabin rocks, and on my palm
  The sifted snow falls, cold and calm.

God! what a power is in the wind!
  I lay my ear to the cabin-side
To feel the weight of those giant hands ;
  A speck, a fly in the blasting tide
Of streaming, pitiless, icy sands;—
  A single heart with its feeble beat—
A mouse in the lion's throat—
A swimmer at sea—a sunbeam's mote
  In the strength of a tempest of hail and sleet!

BENEATH THE PINES

O SUNLESS deeps of northern
    pines !
    O broad, snow-laden arms
        of fir!
Dim aisles where wolves slip to and fro,
    And noiseless wild deer swiftly skirr!
O home of wind-songs wild and grand,
    As suits thy mighty strains, O harp
On which the North Wind lays his hand!
    I walk thy pungent glooms once more
And shout amid thy stormful roar.

As in wild seas a deep is found,
    No wintry tempest stirs, though high
As hills the marching waves upbound
    And break in hissing foam, so I
Walk here secure; though, far above,
    The Storm-king with his train of snows
Sweeps downward from the bitter north,
    And shouts hoarse fury as he goes.

I laugh in tones of ribald glee,
    To see the shaking of his hair,
And hear from out his cloud of beard
    His furious threatenings sweep the air.
The dark pines lower their lofty crests—
    As warriors bow, when chieftain grim
Rides by and shouts his stern behests—
    And with swift answers echo him.

THE STRIPED GOPHER

E IS a roguish little wag!
   He sits like priest, with
      folded hands.
The farm-boy stops behind his drag
   And mocks his whistle where he stands.

The crane in deeps of sunlit sky
   Proclaims the Spring with bugle throat,
Not less the prophecies which lie
   Within the gopher's cheery note.

From radiant slopes of pink and green,
   From warm brown fields his greetings fret.
The eye of hawk is not more keen
   Than his, when danger seems to threat.

He is a cunning little wag!
   He sits and jeers with folded hands.
The farm-boy stoops behind his drag
   And flings a missile where he stands.

THE PRAIRIE TO THE CITY.

O wind of the West, go greet for me
  Those toilers in the city deeps!
Go teach them to be wild and free
  And chainless as the eagle keeps.
Go fill their hearts with hot desire
  To rise above their sooty task,
Go teach them to be wild as fire
  To ask, and compass that they ask!

A HUMAN HABITATION.

The sky was like a low-hung purple disk,
The plain its counterpart.   Eastward, between
These infinite disks of variant purple, the train
Rushed steadily, entering a belt of orange-colored
    sky,
Wherein the spring-time sunlight grew in power.

        Against the glowing band,
A tooth of purple plain upreared, to notch
The otherwise unbroken, splendid sweep
Of intersecting sky and plain.   From it   *
A thin blue smoke arose.

        It was a human habitation.
It was not a prison.   A prison
Resounds with songs, yells, the crash of gates,
The click of locks and grind of chains.
Voice shouts to voice.   Bars do not exclude
The interchange of words.
        This was solitary confinement.

The sun up-sprang,
Its light swept the plain like a sea
Of golden water, and the blue-gray dome
That soared above the settler's shack,
Was lighted into magical splendor.

To some worn woman
Another monotonous day was born.

A RIVER GORGE.

A savage, ragged throat of red
And splintered rocks, through which a dim stream
    flows,
So far beneath, its foam becomes a thread
Of melted silver, poured amid the rose
And orange-tinted lichen-spotted walls.

Across this awful chasm, a jay
Flies dauntlessly, with a ringing cry.
The shuddering soul goes with him on his way,
Made sick with horror, while the high
Cliffs echo with his fearless calls.

ALTRUISM.

A tale of toil that's never done, I tell;
  Of life where love's a fleeting wing
Across the toiler's murky hell
  Of endless, cheerless journeying.
I draw to thee the far-off poor
And lay their sorrows at thy. door.

Thou shalt not rest while these my kind
  Toil hopelessly in solitude ;
Thou shalt not leave them out of mind—
  They must be reckoned with. The food
  You eat shall bitter be,
While law robs them and feedeth thee.

RETURN OF THE GULLS

F AR out upon the treeless sweep
Of sun-smit plain, there come
And go great flights of gulls.
In hot still noon, in roar of wind,
In mist of evening—or in cold clear dawn
They flit in easeful flight above the swash
Of uncut wheat, glittering like flakes
Of snow in flaming sunlight.

They are far from the sea—
How came they here, these children
Of the raw, salt winds of ocean?

All day they wheel and dip
And rise again—complaining, calling
In querulous voices, calling, asking
For something lost.
In keen October dawns
They move in myriads, with the rolling sweep
Of foam-lined waves of water,
Close to the sod in search of food.

At night they settle upon the breast
Of little alkaline lakes and sit and swing
In the soft wash of the water,
And talk of things far off.—
In the winter they hasten south.

For ages they have journeyed thus,
Century by century, while the low land rose
And the water wasted—æons, and still
They came and went.   Generations died,
But the young preserved the custom.
And now, though the land is hot
And the sea is sunk to an alkaline pool,
They come and come, because they bear
Within their faithful brains, the habits
Of a thousand thousand years.

EARLY MAY

BROAD fields of newly-risen wheat
  Whereon lie curving, burnished
    pools
Of smooth rose-golden water.
Across each pond the hylas peep;
A warm soil-scented wind
Moves from the wide, unending spaces
  Of the roseate West, where clouds hang
Like weary birds on wing.

The click of planter, and the shout
Of driver ringing through the air
Adds human presence; while through the rays
Of wide, red-setting sun a slow team moves
A purple shadow on a golden ground.

THE WIND'S VOICE.

I woke far out upon the Kansas sod,
And in the car-eaves overheard,
Close to my ear, as if it called to me,
I heard the sad wind of the plain.
A pushing whisper, the voice
Of a spent runner hoarse with haste,
Burdened with news of the vast
Untrodden west.

On the Mississippi

THROUGH wild and tangled
        forests
The broad, unhasting river flows—
Spotted with rain-drops, gray with night;
    Upon its curving breast there goes
A lonely steamboat's larboard light,
    A blood-red star against the shadowy oaks;
Noiseless as a ghost, through greenish gleam
Of fire-flies, before the boat's wild scream—
    A heron flaps away
    Like silence taking flight.

A BROTHER'S DEATH-SEARCH.

A sadder search you'd hardly plan
　Than a brother seeking a brother's bones,
Seeking the grave of a murdered man,
　　On the plain where the wind like a mourner
　　　moans;
Seeking a skull that the wolves have gnawed,
Bones that the keen-eyed fox has pawed!

Alone on the prairie day by day,
　With keen eyes sweeping the sunny grass
Where the bleaching buffalo skeletons lay—
　　Seeing the hawk's swift shadow pass—
Searching the gullies, amid the stones
For a murdered brother's scattered bones.

Alone on the prairie, night by night;
　In camp where the wild wind, spent and weak,
Comes like a runner hoarse with fright,
　　Whispering a tale he dares not speak—
While the roan at his picket uneasily stirring,
Hears over his head a swift bird whirring.

Alone on the prairie by night, he dreamed,
　Alone on the prairie by day, he spied
The dead man's bones (or so it seemed)
　　A thousand times in his silent ride.
But only the skeleton buffaloes lay
In countless myriads along his way.

Whenever the vulture heavily rose
From a shallow swale with sudden start,
The rider stopped—God!   Who knows,
But the bird is fat with a dead man's heart?—
But only a crib of wild elks' bones
Lay broken and sunken amid the stones.

A sadder search you'd hardly plan
Than a herder seeking a brother's bones,
Seeking a murdered skeleton man
On the plain where the sad wind ever moans—
Seeking the limbs that the wolves have gnawed—
And skull that the keen-eyed fox has pawed.

O, the swift white clouds tell never a tale,
And the wind speaks never a word!
Though it comes in the night with a sobbing wail,
A cry of pain like a wounded bird:
Though wind and cloud may daily pass
Over a skeleton hid in the grass.

SPRING RAINS.

When the snow is sunk
And the fields are bare,
And the rising sun has a golden glare
Through the window pane;
And the crow flies over
The smooth low hills,
And all the air with his calling thrills—
All hearts leap up in song again
To welcome spring and the spring-time rain.

A DAKOTA HARVEST FIELD

O N every side
         The golden stubble stretches,
Looped and laced with silvery spiders' webs.
From stalk to stalk the snapping insects leaping
Add sparks of glittering fire to gold and silver haze.

Their clicking flight the only sounds of living
In all the deepening solemn hush
Of flooding failing light through drooping dreamy
      grain.

The sweet warm light grows every moment richer
Ever more sonorous the damp and hollow air.
And now there comes the clatter of the reaper
And loud and cheery urging of the tired teams.

Around, unseen, the choir of evening crickets
Deepens and widens with the fading dusk,
And distant calls to supper reach across the tangled
      grain.

The over-arching majesty of purple clouds grows
      brighter
Soaring above in seas of green and blue.

A tumbled mountain land of cloud-crags, fired and
   lighted
To glowing bronze, and red and yellow gold.
And through the grain the reaper still goes forward
And still the crickets chirp and insects leap.
And overhead the glory of the sunlight turns to
   gray.

THE NOONDAY PLAIN.

The plain lay under the cloudless sky
In utter and terrible silence.
Not a sound, not a living soul, not a voice
Broke from the russet reach of sod
Save a cricket that cried from the deep
Of his loneliness, like a lost soul.

The grass under foot
Was brittle as glass and dry as dust,
It crumbled to powder under the heel.
A lark's brave voice sounded near, once,
    And was silent with heat.

The light was enormous,
Incredible, world-flooding, insatiable as death!
It was so fierce, the world of sod
Grew dim with over-plus of light—
    It silenced and withered.

The wind came out of the West,
Softly, silently, as if on tiptoe,
And whispered in passing, as though
    It laid a finger on the lip.

The dust of roads arose
Like smoke from crevices of hidden fires,
And sailed across the land
Like banners.   Teams crept beneath
Like weary wingless beetles
    Crawling from cabin to cabin.

Awe and terror rose within
The waiting, watching soul, a horror
Strange and wordless made the heart ache
With wish to fly.   The silence appalled
And the light dazzled.

MIDNIGHT SNOWS

*WITCHERY of the winter
night,
With broad moon shouldering
to the West.*

Sometimes in city streets, at night
I walk alone beneath the trees ;
Before my feet in rustling flight
The west wind sweeps
The midnight snows in untracked heaps,
Familiar, desolate and white.
    Hearing the wind's wild rune,
    I stand and wait with upturned eyes,
    Awed by the splendor of the skies
    And star-trained progress of the moon.

The city vanishes like smoke—
I see the snow-clad prairie gleam
Beneath the magic of the moon,
And age falls from me like a cloak:

I hear the sound of sleigh-bells and the croon
Of loving voices. Through misty night
I hear glad girlish laughter ring,
Clear as some softly stricken string.
The moon is setting toward the West.
The sleigh-bells clash in homeward flight,
With frost each horse's breast is white,
And the big moon sinking at the West!

The watch-dogs bark like sentinels
To hear the passing of the bells.
"O moon, you set to soon, too soon!"
Go sailing on, go sailing slow,
O moon, fast sinking at the West!
The lovers fain would follow thee
Beyond the farthest Western sea.
Too fast the years of girlhood go,
Too soon come toil and all unrest—
Across the diamond-dusted snow
We'd ride forever in your light,
O sovereign of the court of night!

*   *   *   *   *

"Good-night, Lucy!"
"Good-night, Ben!"
The moon is setting at the West!
"Good-night, my sweetheart!" once again
The parting kiss, while comrades wait
Impatient at the roadside gate,
And the red moon sets beyond the West.

IN STACKING-TIME

WITHIN the shelter of the towering
stack
I lie in shadow, blinking at the light;
The sun-light floods the snow-rimmed purple
clouds.
I hear the glorious southern wind
Sweep the sere stubble like a scythe,
While dropping crickets patter 'round me, shaken
down
In flying showers from wind-tossed yellow grain.

O first ripe day of autumn!
O memory half of pain and half of joy!
As if the fate of some dead girl
Haunted my heart, I dream and dream
With aching throat, of dim but unforgotten days.

O wind and light and cool high cloud!
O smell of corn-leaves ripening!   It is so sweet

To lie here, taskless, dumb and rapt
With wordless weight of reminiscent scenes and
    sounds,
Weight of unremembered millions of autumns—
Filled with the wonder of a myriad varied years,
Wonder of winds and woods and rivers, and the
    smell
Of ripened yellow grain and nuts, and the joy
Of sunset rest from toil in dim small fields
In Anglo-Saxon days.

And the shadows wheel and lengthen
Across the level stubble-land, which glows
A mat of gold inlaid with green—
The sun is sunk; sighing I rise to go, and the jocund
    call
Of near-by street-boy breaks the spell
Of cloud and sun and rustling sheaves
And the sweep of the unresting mystical wind—
And overhead I hear the jar and throb
Of giant presses, and the grinding roar
Of ceaseless tumult in the street below
Comes back and welters me again.

PRAIRIE CHICKENS

FROM brown plowed hillocks
    In early red morning,
They woke the tardy sower with their cheerful cry.
    A mellow boom and whoop
    That held a warning,
A song that brought the seed-time very nigh.

The circling, splendid anthem of their greeting,
    Ran like the morning beating
Of a hundred mellow drums—
    Boom, boom, boom!
    Each hillock's top repeating
Like cannon answering cannon
    When the golden sunset comes.

    They drum no more!
Those splendid spring-time pickets,
The sweep of share and sickle
    Has thrust them from the hills;
    They have vanished from the prairie
    Like the partridge from the thickets,
    They have perished from the sportsman,
    Who kills, and kills, and kills!

Often now,
When seated at my writing,
I lay my pencil down
          And fall to dreaming, still,
Of the stern, hard days
Of the old-time Iowa seeding,
When the prairie chickens woke me
          With their chorus on the hill.

A TOWN of the PLAIN

A SHADELESS clump of yellow
blocks,
It stands upon the sod, ringed
With level lands and draped in mist,
Wavering in air so dry, it seems
The very clouds might burn.
A mighty wind roars from the south,
Silencing all other tumult. Its wings
Horizon-wide, welters the grass
And tears the dust and stubble;
And yet the mist remains. Beneath
The wind, flat to earth, teams crawl
Like beetles seeking shelter.
In the glimmering offing
Ricks of grain stand like walls
Of scattered Spanish huts, and like
The easy magic of dreams
Lakes of gray-blue water, bloom
On the hot palpitant plain,
So sweet and fair, the heart
Aches with longing deep as grief.
They mock the eyes a moment
And are gone—and under the wind
The teams crawl on blind with dust,
And faint with thirst.

97

IN THE GOLD COUNTRY

A gray-blue stream that curves
And strikes a high red cliff, lined
With bronze-green pines on the farther side;
Near by a cloud of gray, cold, naked asps—
And far beyond, green-spotted cliffs
Of orange soil, with glittering mountains
Filling the far vista.

HOME FROM WILD MEADOWS

T HROUGH cool dry dust the
wagons rattle,
Their talk subdued and grave
and low.
The horses walk with heads low hanging,
Their footfalls muffled, rhythmical and slow.

Upon the weedy load of rank fall grasses,
I lie and watch the daylight wane,
Hearing the distant thresher's howl and clatter
And cow-bells moving down the dusty lane.

The darkness deepens and the stars appearing
Line out the march of coming night.
And now I catch the sound of farm-yard's bustle
And cross the kitchen's band of friendly, fragrant
    light.

Familiar voices call, the falling neck-yokes rattle,
The pump gives out its welcome squeal.
The barn's gloom swallows team and drivers,
And mother's call to supper rings a hearty peal.

O fragrant waste of autumn grasses!
O prairie by the plowshare torn and rent!
I think of you in days of heat and hurry,
Like traveler in deserts lost and spent.

I wonder if some future world or cycle
Will bring again those radiant seas of bloom,
Wherein all life seemed fair and peaceful,
And bird and beast found generous room.

I'll meet them!   They are not gone forever!
They lie somewhere, those sun-lit prairie lands,
Unstained of blood, possessed of peace and plenty
Untouched by greed's all desolating hands.

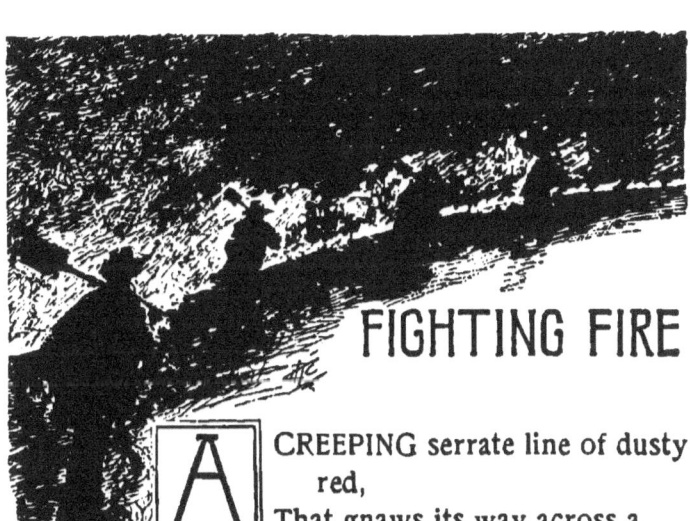

FIGHTING FIRE

A CREEPING serrate line of dusty
  red,
   That gnaws its way across a
   smooth low hill
   Toward long ricks of grain.
Silhouetted against the murky light four men,
With spades at back, stride singly
With unhasting resolute action along the hill
From left to right.   Against the wall
Of red and purple smoke
Each form leans in sharp outline;
The smell of burning hay fills the train;
Then loosely, amply, as a curtain falls
Swinging in the wind, the smoke shuts down
And all is lost to sight.

BOYISH SLEEP.

And all night long we lie in sleep,
  Too sweet to sigh in, or to dream,
Unnoting how the wild winds sweep,
  Or snow clouds through the darkness stream
Above the trees that moan and sigh
  And clutch with naked hands the sky.
Beneath the checkered counterpane
  We rest the soundlier for the storm;
Its wrath is only lullaby,
  A far off, vast and dim refrain.

THE HERDSMAN.

A waste of grasses dry as hair;
Stillness ; insects' buzz, and glare
Of white-hot sunshine everywhere!

The herdsman like a statue sits
Upon his panting horse. While far below
The herd moves soundlessly as a shadow flits,
The weak wind mumbles some mysterious word.

The word grows louder, and a thrill
Of action runs along the hot twin bands
Of steel. A low roar quivers in the ear, and still
No motion else in all the spotted sands.

The roar grows brazen, and a yell
Bursts from an unseen iron throat;
The herdsman's eyes rest on a distant swell,
Whence seems to come the savage welcome note.

Sudden it comes! A crawling, thunderous thing,
A monstrous serpent hot with haste,
The cannon-ball express with rushing swing
Circles the butte and roars across the waste.

The embodied might of these our iron days,
The glittering moving city rushes toward the east,
Bringing for a single instant face to face
Barbaric loneliness and a flying feast.

A roguish maiden from an open window throws
(Or drops) her handkerchief among the cacti spears,
The herdsman plucks and wears it like a rose
Upon his breast, and laughs to hide his grateful
    tears.

Again the waste of grasses crisp as hair;
Stillness; crickets chirp, and glare
Of boundless sunshine everywhere!

RUSHING EAGLE

WITH look so like a lion's
frown,
Savage but sovereign; sombre as Hamlet,
Rebellious as Brutus, desperate as Leonidas,
He fronts the world—the chieftain of a race
Condemned to die.

What tragedy compares with this—
A racial death! Here and there
A chieftain understands. Guiltless as the panther,
Wild as the soul of every wronged
And cheated man, he leaps upon
The wall of circling flame, and falls and dies
Like a trapped wolf.

Here and there a leader goes among
His enemies, and comprehends at last
The height and breadth and pitilessness
Of the flood that sweeps him away.
Then his face settles in lines like those
Of Lear, and his heart swells and breaks,

And in the dim shelter of his tent
He draws his rags about him
    And dies defiantly.

Blessed be his faith in happy hunting-grounds,
For nothing here is left but beggary
And melancholy change.

SEPTEMBER

OOLNESS, ripeness and repose;
The smell of gathered grains
and fruits,
The musky odor of melons everywhere.
The very dust is fruity, and the click
Of locusts' wings is like the close
Of gates upon great stores of wheat.
The gathered grain bleaches in shock,
The corn breathes on me from the west,
And the sky-line widens on and on,
Until I see the waves of yellow-green
Break on the hills that face the snow and lilac
Peaks of Colorado mountains.
        The sun, half-sunk,
Burns through the dusty crimson sky.
Streamers of gold and green soar
In radiating bands, like spokes
Of God's immeasurable chariot wheels,
Half-sunk and falling.   107

The cattle feed about me, here,
Sociably, gnawing the scant dry grass.
I hear their quick short sighs
As one by one they settle for the night.
All is peaceful—save the dull report
Of murderous, quick-repeating gun
Of some insatiate sportsman.

Through the hot haze
The rapid rattle of a hay-rack goes,
And as it passes leaves a trail
Of boyish memories, fading, falling
Like the yellow dust that drifts
Behind the hay-rack's wheels.

THE STAMPEDE.

There's a roar in the depth of the darkness,
There's the thunder of fast-flying feet,
For the herd is awake and blind-rushing,
Made mad with the wind and the sleet.

They stream through the swale like a river,
A flood of black mud on the white
Of the snow-covered ground—and their going
Is wild as an army in flight.

Above the mixed tumult and trample,
Over clashing of horns in the dark—
Over bellowing of bulls, the herder
Lifts voice like the song of the lark.

Round, round in a circle he crowds them,
Singing on, growing hoarse in his song;
Still riding and singing till morning,
Though it's cold and the night-time is long.

He has saved the herd for another,
And what is his hope, his reward?
A dollar a day and a tent cloth
To cover his sleep on the sward.

His owner knows nothing and cares not—
That night he sat at the play
And tossed a bouquet to the danseuse,
Worth twice the brave herder's poor pay.

SPORT.

Somewhere, in deeps
Of tangled ripening wheat,
A little prairie-chicken cries—
Lost from its fellows, it pleads and weeps.
Meanwhile, stained and mangled,
    With dust-filled eyes,
The unreplying mother lies
Limp and bloody at the sportman's feet.

THE
COOL
GRAY JUG.

O cool gray jug that touched the lips
   In kiss that softly closed and clung!
No Spanish wine the tippler sips,
   Or Port the poet's praise has sung,
Such pure, untainted sweetness yields
As cool gray jug in harvest fields.

I see it now! A clover leaf
   Outspread upon its sweating side—
As from the standing sheaf
   I pluck and swing it high, the wide
Field glows with noon-day heat—
The winds are tangled in the wheat.

The myriad crickets blithely cheep;
   Across the swash of ripened grain
I see the burnished reaper creep—
   The lunch-boy comes, and once again
The jug its crystal coolness yields—
O cool gray jug in harvest fields!

THE·GRAY·WOLF

A SHADOWY beast is the
gaunt gray wolf,
And his foot falls soft on
a carpet of spines,
Where the night shuts quick over coverts of firs;
He haunts the deeps of the northern pines.

His eyes are eager, his teeth are keen,
As he slips at night through the brush like a
snake,
Crouching and cringing straight into the wind,
To leap with a laugh on the fawn in the brake.

He falls like a flash on the partridge hen
Brooding her young in the wind-bent weeds,
Or listens to hear, with a start of greed,
The bittern booming from river reeds.

When the chill, snow-laden roaring blast
Swirls round the woodmen's camp at night,
And beats like a spectral bird at the pane,
The men sit circling the broad red light.

Then the story is told by some, of a mate
  Or friend, long lost in the dark and snows,
Who never came back, whose awful fate
  And scattered bones' sepulchre the wolf only
    knows.

And the voices sink to a lower tone,
  As far in the deeps of the sighing pines
A lone wolf's howl, blends with the moan
  Of the wind in the eaves as it sobs and whines.

When the lights are out and the men asleep,
  The wolves, grown bolder, sniff and peer
From the fartherest shades and vainly leap
  Round the tree in the clearing where hang the
    deer;

Till afar in the darkness, signal yells
  And a scurrying chorus of yelps and cries,
To the baffled watch on the clearing tells
  That a frantic deer through the tempest flies.

Oh! a shadowy beast is the gray, grizzled wolf,
  Where his feet fall soft on a carpet of spines;
When the night is dark and the storm sings high
  His voice is abroad in the tossing pines.

He's the symbol of hunger the whole earth through,
  His specter sits at the door of care,
And the homeless hear with a thrill of fear
  The sound of his wind-swept voice on the air.

PLOWING

LONELY task it is to plow!
All day the black and shining
soil
Rolls like a ribbon from the mold-board's
Glistening curve. All day the horses toil
And battle with the flies, and strain
Their creaking harnesses. All day
The crickets jeer from wind-blown shocks of grain.

October brings the frosty dawn,
The still warm noon and cold, clear night,
When stiffened crickets make no sound
And wild ducks in their southward flight
Go by in haste—and still the boy
And toiling team gnaw round by round,
On weather-beaten stubble band by band,
Until at last, to his great joy,
The winter's frost seals up the unplowed land.

A TRIBUTE OF GRASSES.

TO W. W.

Serene, vast head, with silver cloud of hair
Lined on the purple dusk of death,
A stern medallion, velvet set—
Old Norseman, throned, not chained upon thy chair,
Thy grasp of hand, thy hearty breath
    Of welcome thrills me yet
    As when I faced thee there!

Loving my plain as thou thy sea,
Facing the East as thou the West,
I bring a handful of grass to thee—
The prairie grasses I know the best;
Type of the wealth and width of the plain,
Strong of the strength of the wind and sleet,
Fragrant with sunlight and cool with rain,
I bring it and lay it low at thy feet,
    Here by the eastern sea.

MOODS OF THE PLAIN.

The plain has moods like the sea:
It is filled wịth voices and stir
Of wings, when the dust-clouds flee
On the burning wind, and the whirr
Of the crickets is lost in the roar
And the ramp of the southern gale;
When the swash of the wheat runs high,
And the querulous gulls are a-sail
In the pitiless August sky.

    * * *

And the next day rises fair
With a threat of cloud in the West;
And gentle and sweet through the air
Steals the rustle of grain—the winds rest.
But far in the West, the loom
Of cloud is half-concealed
By sheen of sunlight—till the boom
Of thunder like a signal gun
Shatters the veil—and so revealed,
The gathered tempest reels across the sun.

The plain grows dark; like the sea
It holds no shelter. Dwarfed to grains
Of sand, the settlers' cabins cower
Before the tempest, lost in the rain's
Gray wall of dust and spray. The lower
Of clouds makes mid-day night. The crash

Of siege guns would be lost within
The pulsing roar, the illimitable din
Of sprangling lightning, flash on flash.

*   *   *

The roar recedes.   The eager eye
Sees the darkness lighten.   Each glare grows
Each moment dimmer.   A rift
Of western sky a golden crescent shows.
The wind lulls and dripping flowers lift
And watch the daylight come again.
The plain smells sweet, as the skies
Broaden and lighten, and from the trampled grain
The lark's exultant flutings rise.

LOST IN A NORTHER

HERE *are voices of pain*
In the autumn rain,
There are pipings drear in the grassy
waste;
There are lifting swells whose crests arise
Till they touch and blend with the leaden skies
Where massed clouds wildly haste.

I sit on my horse in boot and spur
As the night falls drear
On the lonely plain.   Afar I hear
The cry of goose, and swift wings whirr
Through the graying deeps of the upper air—
Like weary great birds the clouds sail low:
The wind now wails like a woman in woe,
Now mutters and growls like a lion in lair.

Lost on the prairie!
All day alone
With my boyish pride, my swift Ladrone
And the shapes on the shadow my startled
brain cast.   119

Which way is north?   Which way is west?
I ask Ladrone, for he knows best,
And he turns his head to the blast.
He whinnies and turns at my voice's sound,
And then impatiently paws the ground.—
The night's gray turns to a starless black,
And the drifting mizzle and scurrying rack
Have melted afar into rayless night.
The wind, like an actor childish with age,
Plays favorite characters, now sobs with rage,
Now flees like a child in fright.

I turn from the wind (a treacherous guide)
And touch my knee to the glossy side
Of my steaming horse, and the prairie wide
Slips by like the sea under bounding keel;
As I pat his neck and feel the reel
Of his mighty chest and swift limbs' play,
The sorrowful wind voice dies away.

The coyote starts from a shivering sleep
On the grassy edge of a gully deep
And silently slips through the wind-bent weeds;
The prairie hen from beneath our feet
Springs up in haste, with swift wing's beat,
And into the dark like a bullet speeds.

Which way is east?   Which way is south?
Is not to be answered, when dark as the mouth
Of a red-lipped wolf the night shuts down—

I look in vain for a star or light—
Ladrone speeds on with dull thud flight,
His ears laid back in an anxious frown.

The long grass breaks on my horse's breast
As foam is dashed from the billow's crest
    By a keen-prowed ship;
I see it not, but I hear the whip
On my stirrup shield, and feel the rush
And spiteful lash of the hazel brush.

The night grows colder, the wind again—
    Ah. what's that!   I pull at the rein
    And turn my face to the blast—
It was snow on my cheek!   Ay, thick and fast
The startled snows through the darkness leapt,
As massed on the mighty north wind's wing
Like an air-borne army's rushing swing
The awful shadow upon me swept.

I bowed my head till the floating mane
Of my panting horse warmed cheek again,
And plunged straight into the night amain.

＊　　＊　　＊　　＊

Day came and found me slowly riding on
With senses bound as in a chain.
Through drifting deeps of snow, Ladrone,
Dumbly faithful, plodded on, the rein
Flung low upon his weary neck.

I long had ceased to fear or reck
Or death by cold or wolf or snow,
Bent grimly on my saddle bow.

My limbs were numb, I seemed to ride
Upon some viewless rushing tide—
My hands hung helpless at my side.
The multitudinous trampling snows
With solemn, ceaseless myriad din
Swept round and over me; far and wide,
A roaring silence shut the senses in!
Above me through the hurtling shrouds
The far sky, red with morning, glows,
Looked down at times
    And then was lost in clouds.

But were my tongue with poet's spell
Aflame and free, I could not tell
The tale of biting hunger, cold, the hell
Of frenzied thoughts that age-long night!
How life seemed only in my brain; the wind
The foam-white breeze of wintry seas
That roared in wrath from left to right,
Striking me helpless, deaf and blind.
    *   *   *

The third morn broke upon my sight,
Streamed through the window of the room
In which I woke, I knew not how.
Broke radiant in a golden bloom,
As though God smiled away the night!

Like an eternal changeless sea
Of burnished marble lay the plain,
In dazzling, moveless, soundless waste—
Horizon-girt, without a stain.

The air was still.   No breath of sound
Came from the white expanse—
The whole earth seemed to wait in trance,
In hushed expectant silence bound.
And, O the beauty of the eastern sky,
Where glowed the herald banners of the king!
And as I looked with famished eye—
Lo! day came on me with a spring.

Along the iridescent billows of the snow
The sun shot slender, glancing beams—
Like flaming arrows from the bow
They broke on every crest, and gleams
    Of radiant fire
        Alit on every spire
Along the great king's pathway as he came.
    And cloudless, soft, serene as May,
    Opened the jocund day!

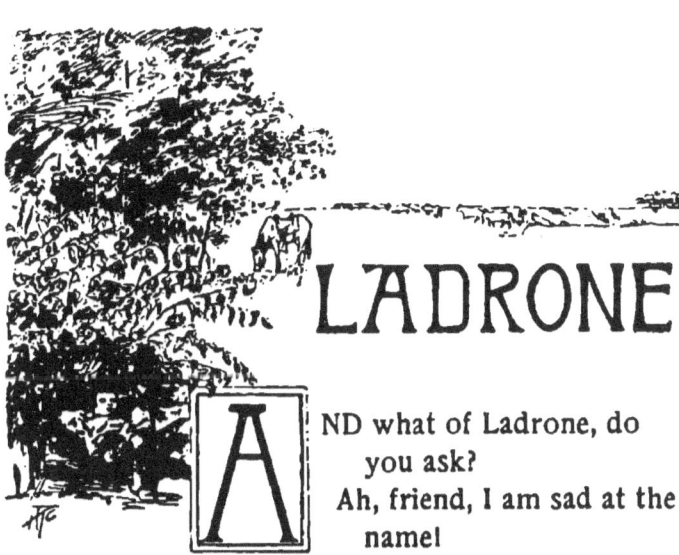

LADRONE

AND what of Ladrone, do
you ask?
Ah, friend, I am sad at the
name!
My splendid fleet roan!—the task
You require is a hard one at best.
Swift as the spectral coyote, as tame
To my voice as a sweetheart—an eye
Like a pool in the woodland asleep,
Brown, clear and calm, with color down deep
Where his brave, proud soul seemed to lie.

Ladrone! There's a spell in the name,
The dank walls fade on my eye—the roar
Of the city grows dim, as a dream;
My spirit leaps up as to soar;
Once more I'm asweep on the plain,
The summer wind sings in my hair;
Once again I hear the wild crane
Crying deep in the shimmering air;
White clouds are adrift on the breeze,
The flowers nod under our feet,

And under my thighs—'twixt my knees,
Again, as of old, I can feel
The roll of Ladrone's vast muscles, the reel
Of his chest—see the thrust of fore-limb
And hear the dull trample of heel !

We thunder behind the wild herd,
My singing whip swirls like a snake;
Hurrah! we swoop on like a bird,
With Ladrone's proud record at stake—
For the shaggy, swift leader has stride
Like the last of a long kingly line.
Her eyes flash fire through her hair,
She tosses her head in disdain,
Her mane streams abroad in the air—
She leads the mad herd of the plain
As a wolf leader leads his gaunt pack
On the slot of the desperate deer—
Their exultant eyes savagely shine!

But down on the leader's broad back
Stings my lash like a rill of red flame—
Huzza, my wild beauty, your best!
Will you teach my Ladrone a new pace ?
Will you break his proud heart with a shame
By spurning the dust in his face ?

The herd falls behind and is lost
As we race neck and neck, stride and stride—
Again the long whip hisses hot
Along the gray mare's glossy side—

Aha, she is lost! She does not respond—
The storm of her speed's at its best—
Now I lean to the ear of my roan
And shout, letting fall the tight rein:
Like a hound from the leash my Ladrone
Swoops ahead—
  We're alone on the plain!

* * *

Yes, alone on the wide, solemn prairie
I ride with my rifle in hand,
My eyes on the watch for the wary
And beautiful antelope band;

Or, sleeping at night in the grasses, I hear
Ladrone grazing near in the gloom.
His listening head on the sky
Comes back, etched complete to the ear.
From the river below comes the boom
Of the bittern, the trill and the cry
Of frogs in the pool, and shrill crickets' chime,
Making ceaseless and marvelous rhyme.

*But what of his fate ? Did he die
When that terrible tempest was done ?
When he staggered with you to the light,
And the fight with the Norther was won ?
Did he live like a guest at your door ?*

No, friend, not so, I—sold him outright.

What, sold your preserver?   He who
Through wind and wild snow and deep night
Brought you safe to a shelter at last!
Did you, when the danger had ended,
Forget your dumb hero, your friend?

Forget?   No, nor shall I—why, man!
It's little you know of such love
As I felt for him—you think that you feel
The same deep regard for your span,
Blanketed, shining, and clipped to the heel.
But my horse was companion and friend,
My playmate, my ship on the sea
Of dun grasses; in all kinds of weather,
Unhoused and hungry sometimes, he
Served me for love, he needed no tether!

No, I cannot forget; but who
Is the master of fortune or fate?
Who does as he wishes and not as he must?
When I sold my preserver, my mate,
My faithfulest friend, man, I wept—
Yes, I own it!   His beautiful eyes
Seemed to ask what it meant, and he kept
Them fixed on me in startled surprise,
As another hand led him away,
And the last that I heard of my roan
Was the sound of his shrill, pleading neigh.

O magic west wind of the mountain !
O steed with the stinging mane!
In sleep I draw rein at the fountain,
But wake with a shiver of pain;
For the heart and the heat of the city
Are walls and prison and chain.
Lost my Ladrone, gone the wild living—
I dream, but my dreaming is vain.

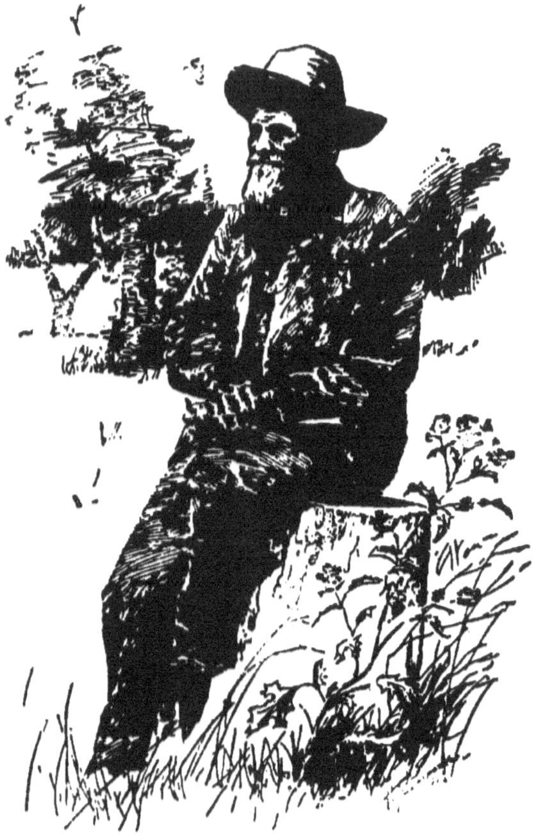

ACROSS THE PICKET LINE.

After we 'd been a-chasin' old Hood
And penned him into Atlanty,
Uncle Billy, doggone him I stood
Around behind us t' make us anty
A-diggin' dirt and a-cuttin' ditches,
F'r days and days I an' top o' that,
We slep', side-arms in our britches
Ready t' fight at the drop o' the hat.

Wal I The rebel pickets got closer 'n' closer
Till blame near we could almost see
The kind o' fellers the Johnnies was,
An' talk as easy as you an' me
Out in the field here plowin' corn
An' gassin' across the dividin' line.
Yessir I An' there we 'd set an' trade off lies
About the war, and provisions, tell
Some feller 'd sing out "Hunt y'r holes I
Give the last man sinjen' hell I "

Wal I Every night we c'd hear 'em sing
" Old Hundred," or " Salvation's Free,"
An' we 'd join in and make things ring—
An' so we got t' know, y' see,
Jest when the Johnnies meant t' shell
'R charge next day, 'r spring a mine
For when they 'd plan 'd t' give us hell
They 'd sing of heaven all 'long the line.

Fact ! Yesslr, sure's y'r born,
  I never see the singin' fail,
Always brought a storm next day
  With bullets flyin' thick as hail,
An' them there Rebs a-scramblin' right
  Straight up to our blessed eyes—
Teeth gritted, faces white—
  An' yellin' fit to raise the skies.

'Fraid ? Not by a darn sight ! They
  Didn't know what the word meant.
No sir—they 'd jest nacherly pray
  An' wherever a man 'ud go, they went;
They wa'n't no discount on their grit,
  And I don't bear 'em any spite.
We met like men, an' settled it,
  And I guess they think it's settled right.

THEN IT'S SPRING

WHEN the hens begin
a-squawkin'
An' a-rollin' in the dust;
When the rooster takes
to talkin',
An' a-crowin' fit to bust;
When the crows are cawin', flockin'
An' the chickuns boom and sing,
Then it's spring!

When the roads are jest one mud-hole
And the worter tricklin' round,
Makes the barn-yard like puddle,
An' softens up the ground
Till y'r ankle-deep in worter,
Sayin' words y'r hadn't orter—
When the jay-birds swear an' sing,
Then it's spring!

LOGAN AT PEACH TREE CREEK.

A VETERAN'S STORY.

You know that day at Peach Tree Creek,
When the Rebs with their circling, scorching wall
Of smoke-hid cannon and sweep of flame
Drove in our flanks, back! back! and all
Our toil seemed lost in the storm of shell—
That desperate day McPherson fell!

Our regiment stood in a little glade
Set round with half-grown red oak trees—
An awful place to stand, in full fair sight,
While the minie bullets hummed like bees,
And comrades dropped on either side—
That fearful day McPherson died!

The roar of the battle, steady, stern,
Rung in our ears. Upon our eyes
The belching cannon smoke, the half-hid swing
Of deploying troops, the groans, the cries,
The hoarse commands, the sickening smell—
That blood-red day McPherson fell!

But we stood there!—when out from the trees,
Out of the smoke and dismay to the right
Burst a rider—His head was bare, his eye
Had a blaze like a lion fain for fight;
His long hair, black as the deepest night,
Streamed out on the wind. And the might
Of his plunging horse was a tale to tell,

And his voice rang high like a bugle's swell;
" Men, the enemy hem us on every side;
We'll whip 'em yet! Close up that breach—
Remember your flag—don't give an inch!
The right flank's gaining and soon will reach—
Forward, boys, and give 'em hell!"—
Said Logan, after McPherson fell.
We laughed and cheered and the red ground shook,
As the general plunged along the line
Through the deadliest rain of screaming shells;
For the sound of his voice refreshed us all,
And we filled the gap like a roaring tide,
And saved the day McPherson died!

But that was twenty years ago,
And part of a horrible dream now past.
For Logan, the lion, the drums throb low
And the flag swings low on the mast;
He has followed his mighty chieftain through
The mist-hung stream, where gray and blue
One color stand,
And North to South extends the hand.

It's right that deeds of war and blood
Should be forgot, but, spite of all,
I think of Logan, now, as he rode
That day across the field; I hear the call
Of his trumpet voice—see the battle shine
In his stern, black eyes, aud down the line
Of cheering men I see him ride,
As on the day McPherson died.

PAID HIS WAY.

No, Steve, I aint complainin' any,
I'll go—if y' think it's right;
I don't ask a single bite n'r a penny
More n'r less 'n jest what's white—
But son, bime by, when the old man's done for,
Jest remember my words to-day.
Y' don't like to have me round h'yere,
But I reckon I've paid m' way!

I was eighty-one last January—
Born in the Buckeye State,
I've opened two farms on the prairie,
An' worked on 'em early and late.
Come rain or come shine, a scrapin' t' earn
Every mouthful we eat, an' want 'o say,
That I never rode in no *free* concern
That I did n't pay my way.

Y'r mother and me worked mighty hard,
How hard you'll never know,
In cold and heat a-standin' guard
To keep off the rain and snow.
The mortgige kep' eatin' in nearer to bone,
And the war it come along too,
But I went—left mother alone
With Sis in the cradle—and you.

Served my time; an' commenced agin
On an Ioway prairie quarter,

An' there I plowed an' sowed an' fenced,
And *nigged* as no human orter,
To raise you young ones and feed m' wife—
Y'r mother scrimped and scrubbed till her hair
    was gray,
And I reckon we paid our way.

No! y'r high-toned tavern *aint* good enough
F'r a man like me to die in,
The work that's made me crooked and rough
Should 'a'earned me a bed to lie in
Under the roof of my only son—
If his wife is proud 'an gay;
For I boosted y' into the place y've won—
O I reckon I've paid my way!

Y'r wife I know is turrible set—
She's mighty hansom to see
I'll admit, but it's a turrible fret
This havin' to eat with me.
She never speaks, and she never seems
To be listnin' to what I say—
But the childern do! *they* don't know yet,
Their grandad's in the way.

I'd know 's you're *very* much to blame
For wantin' to have me go,
But, Steve, I'm glad y'r mother's dead—
'Twould break her heart to know.
She'd say I orter live here,
What time I've got to stay,

For, Stephen, I've travelled for fifty years
An' I've always paid my way.

I ain't a-goin' to bother y' long,
I'll be a pioneerin' further West
Where mother is, and God'll say
Take it easy, Amos, y've earned a rest—
So, Stevie, I want to stay with you—
I want 'o *work* while I stay,
Jes' give me a little sumpin' to do,
I reckon I'll pay my way.

HORSES CHAWIN HAY

I TELL yeh whut! The chankin'
Which the tired horses makes
When you've slipped the harness off'm
An' shoved the hay in flakes
From the hay-mow overhead,
   Is jest about the equal of any pi-any;
They's nothin' soun's s' cumftabul
   As horses chawin' hay.

I love t' hear 'em chankin',
   Jest a-grindin' slow and low,
With their snoots a-rootin' clover
   Deep as their ol' heads 'll go.
It's kind o' sort o' restin'
   To a feller's bones, I say.
It soun's s' mighty cumftabul—
   The horsus chawin' hay.

Gra-onk, gra-onk, gra-onk!
In a stiddy kind o' tone,
Not a tail a-waggin' to 'um,
N'r another sound 'r groan—
Fer the flies is gone a-snoozin'.
Then I loaf around an' watch 'em
In a sleepy kind o' way,
F'r they soun' so mighty cumftabul
As they rewt and chaw their hay.

An' it sets me thinkin' sober
Of the days of '53,
When we pioneered the prairies—
M' wife an' dad an' me,
In a dummed ol' prairie schooner,
In a rough-an'-tumble way,
Sleepin' out at nights, to music
Of the horsus chawin' hay.

Or I'm thinkin' of my comrades
In the fall of '63,
When I rode with ol' Kilpatrick
Through on' through ol' Tennessee.
I'm a-layin' in m' blanket
With my head agin a stone,
Gazin' upwards towards the North Star—
Billy Sykes and Davy Sloan
A-snorin' in a buck-saw kind o' way,
An' me a-layin', listenin'
To the horsus chawin' hay.

It strikes me turrible cur'ous
    That a little noise like that,
Can float a feller backwards
    Like the droppin' of a hat;
An' start his throat a-achin',
    Make his eyes wink that a-way—
They ain't no sound that gits me
    Like horsus chawin' hay!

GROWING OLD.

F'r forty years next Easter day,
  Him and me in wind and weather
Have been a-gittin' bent 'n' gray
  Moggin' along together.

We're not so *very* old, of course!
  But still, we ain't so awful spry
As when we went to singin'-school
  Afoot and 'cross lots, him and I—
And walked back home the longest way—
  An' the moon a-shinin' on the snow,
Makin' the road as bright as day
  An' his voice talkin' low.

Land sakes! Jest hear me talk—
  F'r all the world, jest like a girl,
Me—nearly sixty!—Well-a-well!
  I *was* so tall and strong, the curl
In my hair, Sim said, was like
  The crinkles in a medder brook,
So brown and bright! but there!
  I guess he got it from a book.

His talk in them there days was full
  Of jest sech nonsense—Don't you think
I didn't like it, for I did!
  I walked along there, glad to drink
His words in like the breath o' life—
  Heavens and earth, what fools we women be!

And when he asked me for his wife,
I answered ' Yes ', of course, y' see.

An' then come work, and trouble bit—
Not much time for love talk then!
We bought a farm and mortgaged it,
    And worked and slaved like all possessed
    To lift that turrible grindin' weight.

I washed and churned and sewed—
    An' childurn come, till we had eight
As han'some babes as ever growed
    To walk beside a mother's knee.
    They helped me bear it all, y' see.

It ain't been nothin' else but scrub
    An' rub and bake and stew
The hull, hull time, over stove or tub—
    No time to rest as men folks do.—
I tell yeh, sometimes I sit and think
    How nice the grave 'll be, jest
    One nice, sweet, everlastin' rest !

O don't look scart!   I mean
    Jest what I say.   Ain't crazy yet,
But it's enough to make me so—
    Of course it ain't no use to fret—
Who said it was ?   It's nacherl, though,
    But O, if I was only there—
In the past, and young once more—
    An' had the crinkles in my hair—

An' arms as round and strong, and side
As it was then!—I'd—I'd—

I'd do it all over again, like a fool,
I s'pose! I'd take the pain
An' work an' worry, babes and all.
I s'pose things go by some big rule
Of God's own book, but my ol' brain
Can't fix 'um up, so I'll just wait
An' do my duty when it's clear,
An' trust to Him to make it straight.
— — — Goodness ! noon is almost here,
And there the men come through the gate!

A FARMER'S WIFE.

"Born an' scrubbed, suffered and died."
That's all you need to say, elder.
Never mind sayin' " made a bride,"
Nor when her hair got gray.
　Jes' say, born 'n worked t' death;
　That fits it—save y'r breath.

I knew M'tildy when a girl,
'N a darn purty girl she was !
Her hair was shiny 'n full o' curl,
An' her eyes a kind o' spring-day blue.
　O, I know !　Courted her once m'self,
　Till Brown he laid me on the shelf.

I 've seen that woman once a week
Ever since that very day in church,
　When Ben turned round 'n kissed her cheek
And the preacher knelt to pray.
　I 've watched her growing old so fast—
　Her breath just *flickered* toward the last.

Made me think of a clock run down,
Sure 's y'r born, that woman did;
　A workin' away for old Ben Brown
Patient as Job an' meek as a kid,
　Till she sort o' stopped one day—
　Heart quit tickin' a feller 'd say.

Wasn't old, nuther, forty-six—No,
Jest got humpt, an' thin an' gray,
Washin' an' churnin' an' sweepin', by Joe,
F'r fourteen hours or more a day.
Brats o' sickly children every year
To drag the life plum out o' her.

Worked to death.   Starved to death.
Died f'r lack of air an' sun—
Dyin' f'r rest, and f'r jest a breath
O' simple praise fer what she'd done.
An' many 's the woman this very day
Elder, dyin' slow in that same way.

POM POM PULL AWAY

OUT on the snow the boys
  are springing,
Shouting blithely at their play,
Through the night their voices ringing
  Sound the cry, *Pom, pull away!*
Up the sky the round moon stealing,
  Trails a robe of shimmering white;
Overhead the Great Bear wheeling
  Round the pale stars' steady light.

The air with frost is keen and stinging—
  "*Pom, pom, pull-away!*"
Big boys whistle, girls are singing:
  "*Come away 'r I'll fetch ye 'way.*"
Ah! the phrase has magic in it,
  Piercing frosty moon-lit air,
And in about a half-a-minute
  I am part and parcel there.

147

Across the road I once more scurry,
Through the thickest of the fray,
Sleeve ripped off by Andy Murray—
"Let 'er rip—*Pom, pull-away!*"
Mother'll mend it in the morning,
(Dear old patient, smiling face!)
One more patch my sleeve adorning—
"*Whoop 'er up!*" is no disgrace.

Moonbeams on the snow-crust splinter,
Air that stirs the blood like wine;
What cared we for cold of winter—
Or for maiden's soft eyes' shine?
Give us but a score of skaters
And the game *Pom, pull-away,*
We were always girl-beraters,
Forgot them wholly, truth to say.

O voices through the night air ringing!
O thoughtless happy boys at play!
O silver clouds the keen wind winging
At the cry, *Pom, pull away!*
I sit and dream with keenest longing
For that star-lit magic night—
For my noisy playmates thronging
And the slow moon's trailing light.

GOIN' BACK T'MORRER.

(IN THE CITY.)

I tell ye, Sue, it ain't no use !
I *can't* stay, and I won't—
W'y ! a feller 'd need the widder's cruse
T' live back here an' stan' the brunt
Of all expenses, thick and thin—
Too many men—ain't land enough
T' swing a feller's elbows in—
I 'spose you 'll take it kind a rough
But I 'm goin' back t' morrer!

It ain't no use t' talk t' me
Of whut some other feller owns,
I ain't got no grip at all,
His fire don't warm my achin' bones,
An' then I 'm ust t' walkin' where
There ain't no p'lice 'r pavin' stones—
Of course you 'll think I 'm mighty sick
But I 'm goin' back t' morrer!

Fact is, folks, I *love* the West !
They ain't no other place like home—
They ain't no other place t' *rest*,
F'r mother 'n me but jest ol' Rome,
Cedar County, up Basswood Run—
Lived there goin' on thirty years—
Come there spring o' sixty-one—
An' I 'm goin' back t' morrer !

I tell ye, things looked purty wild
  On that there prairie then !—
We hadn't nary chick n'r child,
  An' we buckled down to work like men—
Handsome land them two claims was
  As ever lay out doors !   Rich an' clean
Of brush an' sloos.   Y'r Uncle Daws
  He used t' say God done his best
On that there land—His level best.

No, I jest can't stand it here,
  Nobow—ain't room to swing my cap.
Ye're all cooped up in this ere flat
  Jest like chickens in a trap—
I 'm mighty sorry, Sue, but I
  Can't stand it, an' mother can't
If *she* was willin' wy I 'd try—
  But I guess we 'll go t' morrer.

'N' when we jest get home agin,
  Back t' Cedar County, back t' Rome,
Back t' Basswood Run an' *bome*,
  Won't the neighbors jest drop in
When we git settled down an' grin
  An' all shake han's—an' Deacon White
Drive up t' laff that laff o' hisn—
  Mother, let's start back t'night !

The corn is jest a-rampin' now—
I c'n hear the leaves a-russlin'—
As they twist an' swing an' bow—
I c'n see the boys a-husslin'
In the medder by the crick
    Forkin' hay f'r all in sight—
An' the birds an' bees s' thick !—
    O we *must* start back t' night !

ON WING OF STEAM.

Into the West
Rain-brightened and fresh as if new
From the Kingdom of God.
Through the wide meadows, dressed
In the glory of sun-lighted sod,
Bright with the green of the grasses,
As the heavens are bright with their blue.

Into the West!
I laugh as we cling
On the green ridges' crest,
I exult and am glad;
I swoop and I swing
Like an eagle on wing
Of the wind—I shout and am mad
With a wild sweet pain
    To meet the plain.

Into the West!
Beneath me the swells
Slip by and are lost,
As the foam-whitened wave
Under keel of a ship, wells
Like a fountain one instant, and tossed,
As with plow, hisses white into spray,
While the boat sweeps away.

Into the West.
The miles fall behind us;
I am filled with wild joy
That earth can not bind us.
A league but a toy
To be played with and tossed
To the winds.   I am part of the pride
And the glory of man,
As onward we sweep
On the cloud-dappled deep
Of the mighty green sea,
In a swift and most marvelous ride
Into the West.

MY PRAIRIES

I LOVE my prairies, they are
mine
From zenith to horizon line
Clipping a world of sky and sod
Like the bended arm and wrist of God.

I love their grasses. The skies
Are larger, and my restless eyes
Fasten on more of earth and air
Than sea-shores furnish anywhere.

I love the hazel thickets and the breeze,
The never-resting prairie winds; the trees
That stand like spear-points high
Against the dark blue sky,
Are wonderful to me. I love the gold
Of newly shaven stubble, rolled
A royal carpet, toward the sun, fit to be
The pathway of a deity.

I love the life of pasture lands, the songs of
    birds
Are not more thrilling to me, than the herd's
Mad bellowing—or the shadow stride
Of mounted herdsmen at my side.

I love my prairies, they are mine,
From high sun to horizon line.
The mountains and the cold gray sea
Are not for me, are naught to me.

MIDWAY ON THE TRAIL.

Fifty thousand miles in America!
Fifty thousand miles of hill and plain,
Of levels by the sea, of wooded land,
Circling loopings of a restless life.

Midway on the trail!
Here at the end of my book, I rest,
And memories throng upon me—
Memories wide as seas, cool as streams,
And lofty as the serrate rim
Of mountain chains.   Memories of fields
And pleasant groves, rushing winds, and nights
Of moon-lit splendid September.—
Imperishable memories of mighty days,
    Circling before me.

O those days!   They come and come
Like thronging songs both sweet and sad.
Days on the Dakota plain, in spring
When the sod is green and velvet-smooth,
Days on the mountains alone with the eagles.
Days on the Mississippi, feeling the jar and throb
Of the engine's splendid beam,
Days by the shining Western sea—
O splendor and power of days.

All America is there!
Memories of the Eastern sea, hearing the clang
Of the lonely, dolorous bell-buoy's tongue,

Memories of New England meadow lands,
Memories of vineyards in Ohio, close beside—
I recall orchards in Delaware and the pink
Of peach-trees on the slopes of Lookout Moun-
tain.
Memories of sinuous trails that braid
The breasts of mountains. I feel again
The shivering awe with which I faced
The Spanish Peaks across the level land.
Memories of orange orchards follow
And the sunless deeps of Alabamian swamps,
And the gleam of fire-flies in the hot still night.
Thronging thick and orderless as dreams,
Pictures come, looped on the thread
      Of shining, winding trails.

      I see once more
King Shasta's violet-and-silver crown
Set high against the winter stars,
Illimitable as pride and cold as death.
St. Helen's rises, a glorious moon
Above deep-purple seas of trackless woods,
A soaring semi-circular dome of rose-and-silver
Lit by the flaming sunset light,
      Marvellously beautiful.

I descend again the mountain trail
Toward a moon-lit mystery of land and sea
Outspread below—the canon water calls—
I smell the lemon-blooms, and oranges

Spilled everywhere beneath the trees.
Wild voices echo leaping from cliff to cliff.
The purple landscape darkens swiftly, and lights
    below
Glitter to stars above.
    O God! How beautiful!

    Memories of skies,
Cloudless cobalt skies of level lands,
Where only sun and sand are seen—
Radiant skies of Arizonian deserts.
Californian skies of winter—
Gray skies where the eucalyptus trees
Toss in warm unending rain.
Memories of skies as blue as wrinkled seas
At mid-day, when the winds blow.
    Sunny skies,
Arching some silent Mexican town,
Where dark-skinned children play
Untroubled games before the walls
    Of crumbling Spanish missions.

I drift on Columbia's cold gray water;
I see the fir-clothed rimy peaks burst
From the clouds, three thousand feet
Above the narrows, where the river
Churns itself to foam upon the lichen-spotted
    rocks.
I ride through terrible forests, in gray
Thick-falling rain, ride and ride,

Shadowed by clinging gray-green moss;
Feeling the drip of wet, wind-shaken firs,
Lost in wastes of giant ferns,
    Where the wild deer feeds.

The sunrise blooms again
On the glorious Dakota sod.
I plant my stake on untracked land,
Thrilled with the wonder and marvel of it.
I hear the gabble of weary geese at sunset,
As they pass close to earth, hungry, and timid.
I hear once more the jovial shout
Of jubilant landseeker, and see
The cranes dancing in shadowy row
Beside the shallow pool.
Over me the stars bloom out,
And on my blanket falls the frost
    Of the clear midnight.
        O the irrevocable past!

    Other scenes come back.
I walk behind the seeder on the mellow sod
Of Iowan prairies, warm with sun.
Around and over me goes the northward flight
Of millions of water-fowl; gophers whistle;
I trace the awful circle of the calling crane
Circling the sun in his flight. I hear
The chorus of the prairie chicken.
I toil on in the red sunset.

Harvest days follow.
The flaming sun rides high
Above the gently moving fields of wheat
Stretching to the sky's dim circling rim.
I hear the purring reaper's far-off threat.
The sheaf crackles again under my knee,
My aching muscles roll and swell and strain;
The joy of physical strength fades away.
The sun declines, the dew falls,
The level rays of light stream
In unspeakable glory over the wheat;
The crickets call in rapid repartee,
The darkness sweeps swiftly from the east
I stumble homeward, while the horses pass
With heads wearily down-hanging—
The sun sets on harvest days!

September comes,
And with it a roaring wind, hot and dry.
A magnetic, splendid southern wind.
Stacks of grain arise like plants of sudden growth
The corn grows sere and dry, the air
Is full of smell of ripening grain, the moon
Is like a silver boat in sapphire seas.
I walk behind the plow on still
October days when the frost melts slowly
From the shadowed leaves.
The skies grow gray with snow
And winter comes!

Wild winter days rush over me.
I see the woods teams slowly pass,
I hear the low sweet jingle of the bells,
The water drops from southern roofs,
The mid-day sun, dazzlingly beautiful,
Spills blue shadows on the unstained snow.
I hear the shouts of skaters in the swales,
I hear the shouts of axemen in the pines,
The wolf slips by
Swift as winter days,
 In deep Wisconsin woods.

I am on the prairies again;
Seamless domes of cloud
Rise in the West, heavy with wind and snow.
Once again the swift snow, slides
Fitfully, menacingly, and the Norther comes,
Bringing sun-set at mid-day; and the weight
Of all winter is on the pitiless blast.
Blind and desperate I ride and ride!
I lie beneath a shanty roof and hear
The high-keyed, frenzied, piping, persistent howl
Of the midnight wind, and the rushing roar
Of the streaming, lashing snows.
There is no earth, no sky,
 Nothing but snow.

 Snow!
I saw it rest on sheltering arms of fir,
I saw it lay old and sullen, in mountain pass

Ten thousand feet above the sea. I saw
It saffron with the wind-blown sands
On old Mount Ouray, where the wind
Had died at last of cold and weariness.
Across a waste of lesser hills
The College Group soars, a wall
Of silver based in purple.

    Snow!
I ride behind a swift young horse
Beneath broad Iowan oaks; the bells
Make the clear night musical, the sky,
Low-hung, splendid, is frosty with stars,
And the moon sails on in silence;
Her wake of light lies on the crusted snows,
But she sails on and on beyond the skies,
Beyond the land of youth and love,
:nto the land of mystery
Beyond the fartherest West.

    O glorious days!
I cannot lose you. I will not.
Here in the current of my song,
Here I sweep you all together,
The harvest of a continent, the fruit
Of a thousand days of travel.
Here where neither time nor change
Can rob me of you. So
When I am old, like a chained eagle
I can sit and dream and dream

Of splendid spaces and the gleam
Of rivers, and the smell
    Of prairie flowers.

So I can live again
Above the clouds, and on
The reeling horse, hear the wind
Roaring from dark and wooded canons.
So, when I have quite forgot
The heritage of books
I still shall know
The splendor and majesty
    Of my native land.

HERE ENDETH THE BOOK NAMED PRAIRIE SONGS
.·. PRINTED BY JOHN WILSON & SON .·. AT THE
UNIVERSITY PRESS .·. IN CAMBRIDGE .·. FOR
STONE & KIMBALL .·. THE YEAR OF OUR LORD
MDCCCXCIII